HAUNTED DOLLS

Written & Illustrated By Davina Rush

OTHER COLORING BOOKS
by Davina Rush

Creatures of Greek Mythology

Creatures of Classic Horror

Famous Painters in Art History

Alice in Wonderland

Haunted Dolls

and more to come!

Keep up to date on the latest publications at

www.DavinaRush.Com

As with everything in my life,

this book is dedicated to my two beautiful daughters

HAILEY AND MELINA

CONTENTS

HAUNTED DOLLS

Written & Illustrated By Davina Rush

INTRODUCTION

Most all of us have held a doll close to our heart at least once in our life; clinging to this inanimate friend as if it were absolutely real, confiding our deepest secrets into their cotton stuffed ears, falling asleep with them in our arms so full of perfect trust. However, in very rare cases, this innocent plaything has taken on a much more sinister role, spreading fear rather than joy within the household. Here, within these pages you will read about a collection of such dolls—haunted dolls, who reportedly plagued their owners with acts of mischief, chilling voices, and even physical violence. Prepare yourself. You may find the things that you are about to read quite disturbing, especially since you most likely have at least one doll somewhere in your own house right at this very moment; small beady eyes watching your every move as you read these words. If this thought terrifies you, or if you scare easily—close this book now

NOTE: The author has researched the material contained within this book but does not claim to be an expert on any of the subject matter presented here. The stories that surround each of the dolls included in this book vary widely from source to source, making the facts *very* hard to flawlessly confirm. However, for entertainment purposes, the author has collected the most popular versions of the stories for your enjoyment. In addition: all illustrations within this book are creative interpretations of the original subject, not exact replicas of the original dolls. Photographs of the original dolls can be found in the reference section of this book or, more extensively, online.

Parental discretion is advised

ANNABELLE

With her bright red yarn hair, whimsical triangle nose and a cheerful, stitched smile, this childhood icon became quite popular and stayed that way for many years. Making her first appearance on the market in 1915, Raggedy Anne was further promoted with the 1918 book that featured the doll and her brother, Raggedy Andy. They were a hit! The two would later find their way into even more hearts with the introduction of their animated television series in 1988. With this, Raggedy Anne and Andy quickly became a beloved household name and treasured friend to many children.

In 1970, over 50 years after the toy's initial debut, Raggedy Anne remained just as popular among children, as well as with the adults who had grown up with her. One such adult was a young nurse by the name of Donna. Her mother knew how she had adored the character as a child and so presented her with an antique Raggedy Anne doll for her birthday. Donna was overjoyed with the gift, eagerly taking it back to the apartment that she shared with her roommate, Angie. The two girls fawned over the doll for a bit before settling her into the décor of their home, though she would not stay put for long.

Strange things began to happen almost immediately after the doll came into their lives. It started small, with incidents that could easily go unnoticed; the doll's legs being crossed or uncrossed when they had not been left that way, and other slight changes in position; minor things that you might walk past every day in your own house and not even realize. However, the girls *did* notice and began to pay closer attention to little Anne. As they observed the ragdoll more intently, she started to act out, thriving on their attention. She quickly progressed from simple tricks to more noticeable feats, mysteriously moving to completely different locations throughout the apartment or standing when she had been left sitting. On one occasion, the girls even claimed that the doll had moved into another room with the door closed and that they had found droplets of what appeared to be blood on her dress. Finally, as if these occurrences were not enough, the doll began leaving notes on parchment paper, with the words, "Help us"—to which both Donna and Angie claimed they had never even owned parchment paper.

After months of torment, Donna and Angie finally decided to contact a professional medium for answers, feeling that the dolls' behavior must be of supernatural origins. Through the medium, the girls were put into contact with the soul of seven-year-old Annabelle Higgins, a young girl who had been found dead on the very property where their apartment building now stood. The spirit of the child told her sad tale and then pleaded with the two women to allow her to stay and inhabit the doll that they had so lovingly cared for. Feeling sorry for the child, the girls agreed. However, they would soon find out that Annabelle was not at all what she had claimed to be.

Not long after their introduction to young Annabelle, things got much worse. Lou, a friend of Donna and Angie's, felt very strongly that the doll was evil and that they should get rid of her immediately. Apparently, Annabelle did not agree with Lou at all. After stating his opinions about the doll, Lou reported having awakened to Annabelle standing at his feet where he lay paralyzed and at her mercy. He claimed that the doll slowly glided up his body until it was at his throat, choking him until he blacked out. In another instance, Lou awoke with multiple claw marks slashed across his chest. Clearly Annabelle did not like being talked about behind her back and she most definitely did not plan on leaving the girls without a fight.

As the incidents became progressively violent, Donna and Angie realized that they were dealing with something much more sinister than the spirit of a little girl. They again decided to seek help for their situation, this time calling on a priest. After explaining the doll's disturbing behavior, the priest felt compelled to consult with another priest for a second opinion. Ultimately, both priests decided to call on Edward and Lorraine Warren, the self-proclaimed paranormal investigators, and demonologists.

The Warrens came to Donna and Angie's apartment to further investigate the doll for themselves. After their consultation, the Warren's concluded that the presence controlling the doll was not that of the young Annabelle after all, but rather an inhuman entity—a demon. They explained that the demon had been using Anabelle and the doll all along as a pawn to get closer to and lower the defenses of the women. He had been using their sympathies and fears to hold the two in his thrall, in hopes of possessing one of them. If the priests and the Warrens had not come into the picture when they did, who knows what might have happened next.

To end Donna and Angie's nightmare, the two priests cleansed the house with special in-depth prayers and the Warrens physically removed the doll from the house. Annabelle was then placed in the Warrens' home collection, locked away in a special glass case. To this day, the Annabelle doll is routinely blessed by priests to keep the unholy entity that is attached to it suppressed.

ROBERT THE DOLL

When I was a little girl, around four or five-years-old, I had a doll as tall as I was, with blonde hair and blue eyes, just like me. I absolutely adored her. We played together for hours on end and I would talk to her as if she were a real friend, even sharing clothes with her as we wore the same size (photo in back of this book). Many children had such dolls, large or small, that they bonded closely with in their youngest years. This is such a common and innocent thing all around the world—a child and their doll. However, some instances are a bit more unusual and, in rare cases, even scary.

At the age of four, Robert Eugene Otto (Gene) of Key West Florida was presented with such a doll. It was a very special gift, handcrafted with fabric and stuffed with wood shavings, having traveled all the way from Germany. Gene loved his new companion, naming him Robert, after himself, and even giving him one of his own outfits; the sailor suit that he still wears to this day. The two spent hours together as Gene took him everywhere, playing and bonding within the special magic of imagination.

At first, Gene's parents only noted the small instances, such as Gene blaming the doll for things that he had gotten into trouble for; overturned furniture, broken toys— the usual childhood mischief. They didn't think overmuch about these incidents, discounting it as mere child's play, until things took a much darker turn. The parents claimed that on more than one occasion they awoke to Gene screaming in the night and that, after racing to the child's room, they would find young Gene struggling to hold the doll pinned to the floor. This, of course, gave them cause to worry and so they tried to put some distance between the two, though it proved almost impossible to keep them apart.

Gene eventually grew up, maintaining his relationship with "Robert" for the entirety of his life, taking care of the doll until his own death in 1974. After his passing, Eugene Otto's childhood home, known as "The Artist's House", was purchased by Myrtle Reuter. With the acquisition of the home Ms. Reuter also inherited an unexpected tenant--Robert the doll, who had been tucked away in the attic, though not as you might think. Rather than being packed away in storage, it would be more accurate to say that he was 'housed' in the attic, as the space had been set up with small furniture proportionate to the doll with a modest collection of toys for him to play with. Apparently, Otto's wife had not been comfortable with the doll, so Otto had set up the room in the attic to keep both his wife and Robert happy. Reuter found the doll in the attic room and chose to keep him for a time, moving him downstairs, not yet realizing what she was in for. She claimed that Robert soon began moving around the house on his own, from room to room, and that she would sometimes hear a child giggling in the halls. She tolerated the incidents for a time, but after twenty years of endless and disturbing shenanigans, Reuter finally decided to donate Robert to a museum in 1994. "The Artist's House", which Eugene had grown up in and lived in as an adult with the notorious doll, is still standing at 534 Eaton Street in Key West Florida and is open to the public as a bed and breakfast where you can even sleep in Robert's old room—if you dare.

Robert the doll is now over 100 years old. He remains at the *Fort East Martello Museum* in Key West Florida, where he is carefully preserved in a glass case. Visitors from all over the world travel to the museum every day to get a look at the haunted toy, and some people even write letters to him. Most often these letters contain pleading apologies from people who feel that they must have offended Robert in some way when they visited, having encountered great amounts of misfortune after their encounter with the doll. He has been blamed for many things, from car accidents and broken bones, to job loss and divorce. Apparently, he does not tolerate being disrespected.

Robert the doll has been featured on numerous tv show documentaries, telling the story of his relationship with the Otto's, as well as the unusual occurrences that have happened since he came to the museum and within his previous home on Eaton Street. One such documentary tells the story of a young museum curator who was so afraid of the doll that she quit her job immediately after an experience with him. She explained that the doll had recently been checked, cleaned and put safely back into his display case the evening before. Then, the very next morning, when she arrived at work, she noticed that Robert's feet were quite dirty and that there were small footprints all around the glass case. She then claimed to have heard a tap on the glass case and a giggle from inside. Already Terrified, the curator turned to look at the doll just in time to see him move. The terrified woman ran from the room and vowed never to return.

Not only has Robert the doll been featured in many documentaries, he has also inspired some very well-known movie characters. The most memorable cinema likeness is said to be that of the notorious Chucky doll. Though Robert the doll did not murder anyone, he did terrify his owners, forever taunting and toying with them and anyone else who came near. But maybe he really didn't mean any harm with his mischievous ways, and if he could speak, perhaps he might simply ask—"Wanna Play?"

THE ISLE OF THE DOLLS

Perhaps far more disturbing than one single haunted doll is a collection of hundreds. Especially when they all reside on an abandoned island, rotting, blackened with filth and covered in cobwebs; their vacant eyes watching every person who dares step foot in their domain.

The Isle of the Dolls, or *Isla de las Muñecas*, is located along the channels of Xochimilco, just south of the center of Mexico City. Said to be one of the most haunted places in Mexico, the channels are saturated with tales of death and the darkest of despair. So many people have died tragically in this place throughout history, particularly during the Mexican Revolution when masses of people were slain, their bodies were irreverently dumped into the river. Because of this dark history and the many tales of ghostly encounters, most of the locals fearfully avoid the place entirely. Some even claim that many of the drowning deaths are caused by vengeful souls pulling people under the water.

No one can say if the countless ghost stories are true, but the creepiness of this island is a certain fact. Hundreds of dolls swing limp from the tree branches overhead where they have hung for many years, or on the walls of the island cabin where they are bound in place by nails or rope. Dolls of every variety, crawling with bugs and the spirits that cling to them, are there to greet anyone who dares step foot onto their shore. However, perhaps even more disturbing than the mere presence of these dolls is the tale behind their existence.

As the story goes, in the early 1950s a man called Don Julian came to the island seeking solitude from the outside world, solitude that he was not destined to find. Directly after moving to the cabin, some say on the same day, the man witnessed a young girl drowning in the nearby river. He attempted to save the child but, sadly, he failed, and the girl perished before his eyes. Consumed with guilt, the man's heart broke for the little one—although his sorrow would soon turn into fear and unrest as he realized that the girl was not gone from this world after all. Some part of her had remained.

Not long after the child's passing, a small doll washed ashore. Don Julian was certain that this toy belonged to the little girl. He became increasingly convinced of the doll's origins as he began hearing the disembodied cry of a child with the dolls' arrival. He felt very strongly that the sobbing belonged to the soul of the drowned girl, lost on the island—apparently without her doll. To appease the discontented spirit, the man hung her doll in a tree near where the little girl had departed this world, offering the treasured poppet back to her rightful owner. He had hoped that the toy would calm her loneliness, but his efforts were to no avail as the little girl continued to cry night after night, endlessly tormenting the man. Because of this, every day for many years, Don Julian would bring yet another doll to offer the sorrowful child—and another, and another—until eventually the island was fully populated in all directions with every variety of doll.

Don Julian lived on the island for the remainder of his life, finally leaving this world after fifty years of servitude to the soul that had relentlessly haunted him. His body was found by his own brother in the exact same spot where the young girl had drowned. He had spent so many years of his life on the island, continually gifting dolls to the restless soul of the child, hoping to ease her grief. However, the spirit of the little girl never stopped her nightly lamenting with all of his gifts, nor even after Don Julian's death. To this day, visitors continue to report the sound of a crying child, while others claim to have felt a disembodied hand touching them, and still others claim to have seen the dolls themselves moving in unnatural ways or the ghostly image of a child roaming the quiet shores.

After his death, the island was once again deserted; abandoned to its ghosts. The only thing that remains in this place is Don Julian's two cabins and the innumerable decaying dolls that have claimed the island for their own. The locals will not inhabit the island, but often guide tourists to the much sought-after location. One particular doll that Don Julian named Augustanina has become a shrine of sorts, where pilgrims continuously leave offerings of money, candies, toys etc.

LeTTA Me Out

Imagine a small town in New South Wales, Australia, where an old abandoned farmhouse stands eerily quiet—a house that has been the subject of countless spooky stories, terrifying kids for generations. Houses such as this exist all over the world, probably even in your own neighborhood; but very few have held a secret such as this one. In this particular house there lay a hidden resident that would not be found for decades, until a man named Kerry Walton and his brother returned to their childhood neighborhood in the 1970s, exploring the dilapidated old structure.

The Walton brothers had been curious and wary of the old house for most of their lives, as local rumors claimed the place to be haunted. They had always avoided the house, like everyone else-- until one night, as adults, when they faced the fear that had stayed with them for so long. On an adventurous whim and a dare, the two decided to go hunting for antique treasures in the old farmhouse. They looked around the property together finding nothing of real value, that is, until they ventured underneath the house itself. The two explored the crawlspace beneath the old structure in hopes of finding hidden treasure, but instead, to their horror, they found what they thought to be the body of a small child. Driven by their curiosity and concern, the two moved closer to inspect the body. Thankfully, they found that it was not a child, but rather a large wooden doll lying alone in the dark, his oversized smile reflecting in the beam of their flashlight.

After finding the antique doll, the brothers were satisfied and decided to call it a night. They left for home, taking their treasure with them, tucked away in a sack in the back seat of their station wagon. As they drove away, the brothers noticed that the night lights playing on the sack made it seem as if the doll were moving inside. Kerry shrugged it off as his brother jokingly said, "Letta me out!", as if he were the doll asking to be set free. The joke stuck and so they named the doll *Letta Me Out*, or *Letta* for short.

Their family was immediately apprehensive about the doll when the brothers brought him home. Its wide eyes, scowling brows and sinister smile, along with his unsettling origins did not set easy with anyone in the household. And their fears were soon validated as the doll began moving around the house on his own within the first few days, appearing and disappearing from locations without anyone touching him. People began complaining about feeling sick or faint around the doll; and dogs would bark, trying to bite at him.

Eager to be rid of the disturbing artifact and curious if perhaps they could make some money from it, the brothers decided to have the doll appraised and analyzed by experts. After careful inspection, Letta was determined to be over 200 years old, having spent at least 60 of those years hidden away beneath the old farmhouse. Experts also believe the doll to be of Romanian origins since its features seem to be made in that likeness. The experts also determined that the doll was crafted with real human hair on his head, something that only led to *more* questions and concerns.

After having the doll evaluated through the Australian Museum in Sidney, Kerry soon found a buyer who offered him four-hundred dollars for the antique. In desperate need of the money, he loaded Letta into his car and went to meet the man, determined to sell the poppet and be rid of him. However, when he arrived, he found himself staring at the doll, unable to remove him from the car. He felt that Letta had some strange hold on him, not allowing them to part ways. Kerry decided then that he could not sell the doll. After this incident, Kerry's other antiques and collectables began to sell better than ever, and he couldn't fight the feeling that Letta had something to do with this remarkable success. Since then, Kerry has been offered up to ten-thousand dollars for the doll, though he has refused, saying that Letta is **not** for sale.

After many strange occurrences and to further their investigation of the doll, the brothers decided to bring him to multiple psychic mediums. Each one claimed that the doll was inhabited by the spirit of a young boy who had drowned and whose likeness the doll had been fashioned in. It was common in some cultures to create such dolls when a loved one passed too young. As such, it is believed that Letta harbors not only the energy of the child whose likeness he was made in, but also the sorrow and anger of the man who made the doll in his terrible grief. During these revelations with the psychic medium, Letta was witnessed to wriggle in her lap and to turn his head on his own, just before a lightbulb blew in the room, seemingly confirming what was said.

Fortunately for the Walton family, and despite his creepy appearance, Letta is believed to be inhabited by a good-natured spirit who brings good luck to their family and to anyone who meets him. Because of this, he has made quite a few friends over the years and even has his own Facebook page, as well as a few documentaries that you can view, like the YouTube video "Letta Me Out on State Affair 1981" and "Letta Me Out on Extra 2002".

OKIKU

Eikichi Suzuki absolutely adored his little sister, two-year-old Okiku. He always doted on her and enjoyed surprising her with various little gifts. So, in 1918, when he had come across a particularly beautiful doll while out shopping one day, Eikichi knew instantly that he had to have this prize for little Okiku. Made of fine porcelain, dressed in a beautiful kimono, with black eyes made of polished beads and dark shoulder-length hair, the doll was truly a treasure that any little girl would love. Of course, little Okiku was overjoyed with the gift. She adored the doll, quickly becoming inseparable from her new friend. They were always together night and day—that is, until tragedy struck the Suzuki family just one year later.

Okiku had come down with a terrible fever, and though her family had done all they could to help her, in the end, her little body could not endure. Okiku Suzuki died at a mere three years old. Her family, in shock and devastation, looked on the tiny coffin and to this doll that their daughter had loved so dearly, their grief immeasurable. It is said that the family had planned to lay Okiku's special doll to rest with her on that day, knowing how much she had adored the toy, but ultimately decided instead to seat the doll on the family altar in their home, in remembrance of the beloved child.

The doll was placed reverently on the family altar, along with photos of little Okiku and other various items that were special to the Suzukis. This is a common practice in Japanese culture, a simple and yet beautiful gesture to honor loved ones who are far away or no longer with us. The altar and the doll were a peaceful and loving reminder of their little Okiku— until a few months later when the family noticed something very strange about the doll. Where they knew that the doll had always had short, shoulder length hair, she now had hair down to her waist. It was impossible, and yet somehow the doll's hair seemed to be growing! Her family quickly came to believe that the toy was alive in some way and that perhaps the spirit of their little girl was connected to it or perhaps even *inside* of the doll.

The Suzukis cared for the doll in honor of their daughter, claiming that the hair continued to grow and grow, even as they cut it regularly. They kept the doll in this way until 1938 when they finally decided to move away—without the doll. Packing up the contents of their home for the move, they were afraid to pack up the doll or to move it too far from the only home that their daughter had ever known. They were afraid that by moving the doll, Okiku's soul would become lost. So, in order to keep her close to the original family home, they decided to place the doll in the care of the nearby Mannenji temple.

The Suzukis went to the priests at the temple and asked if they would take the doll. They informed the temple priests of the doll's growing hair and told them of their belief that Okiku's spirit was inhabiting the toy. Because of this, the head priest vowed to look after the doll himself, to observe and witness any miracle that might occur.

Indeed, over the years, the priests of the temple claim to have witnessed the miraculous growth of the doll's hair, though many people believe that it is no more than a hoax. Samples have been taken of the doll's hair and verified to be of human origins, however, this does not prove that the growth is a supernatural occurrence. It has been common practice over many generations and in many cultures to use real human hair in doll making; either as an aesthetic feature or to honor a loved one who has died. So, it is highly likely that the doll always had human hair and was simply made this way. Although, real human hair or not, by all rights, it should *not* still be growing.

Regardless of what people believe or do not believe, the priests have continued to care for Okiku's doll even unto this day. They periodically cut the doll's hair when it grows too long and keep her well preserved in her little display box. She is available for public view at the temple on Hokkaido island, in Japan. She is kept there in a small wooden display box on her own small altar, surrounded by photos of her hair at various lengths.

Perhaps Okiku's doll truly is haunted, or perhaps it is only a hoax. Either way, this is probably one of the most loved and well-cared-for dolls on the planet. The priests tend to her daily as she sits on her little altar, and people visit her from around the world, saying prayers for the child who may or may not be attached to the plaything.

PUPA

Children all over the world, for as long as mankind can remember, have owned dolls. They cling to them as a familiar friend, as a trusted confidant, pouring every secret, every emotion into these little poppets. They cry into their synthetic hair at night when they are frightened, they feed them pretend food when they imagine they must be hungry, they take them on adventures, not wanting to leave their beloved companion behind. In a way, the child breathes life into this inanimate object-- sometimes to a disturbing degree. Pupa is one such doll, having been loved so much that she quite took on a life of her own.

A unique creation from the very beginning, Pupa was nothing like the mass-produced dolls of today's toy industry. In fact, she was quite singular, having been custom-made to look like the little girl she was intended for, even down to the most intimate detail, using the child's own hair in its making.

As the story goes, in the early 1920s, Pupa was hand-made for a little girl in Trieste, Italy as a special gift. Standing around fourteen inches tall, the doll's body and light blue dress were made of felt in the likeness of her owner. Her hair was even made from actual clippings of the little girl's hair to make them more so the matching pair with their blonde curls and blue eyes mirroring each other. A special gift indeed!

And what little girl wouldn't love such a treasure-- a tiny replica of themselves, a best friend with an already familiar face. The two quickly became close, spending all of their days together, from the time that Pupa entered the little girl's life in the early 1920's until her death in 2005.

However, the story of Pupa did not end with her owner's death. In fact, it only got stranger. The original owner had always claimed that Pupa had a mind of her own and would actually talk to her. She truly felt that the doll was alive in some way, calling Pupa her best friend and even claiming that the doll had saved her life once. The family thought this was all nonsense and dismissed her stories—that is, until the woman died, and they inherited the doll.

In their care, the family placed the beloved doll in a glass display case for safe keeping. They kept her in this way to honor their grandmother, respecting her deep love for the toy. Their intentions in this method of storing the doll were well-meaning; however, this did not seem to be acceptable to Pupa. It soon became unmistakably evident that the doll did not like being confined in this way and would not quietly tolerate the mistreatment.

The family, who had once dismissed the seemingly tall tales surrounding the doll, were now faced with very strange occurrences that they could not explain. They reported such things as the glass of the display case mysteriously fogging up. This alone is a phenomenon that might be easily explained with scientific answers—but then writings would appear on the steamy glass, saying things such as, "Pupa hate!" Clearly, this abandoned dolly was trying to communicate her distaste for the unjust confinement. She went further in her pleas for freedom, pushing things around in the small space, rearranging her tiny prison in an angry tantrum. The family even claimed to have repeatedly heard tapping sounds on the glass, as if the doll were knocking, pleading to be let out. And on a few occasions, they told of how Pupa would escape her case, happily placing herself somewhere more agreeable within the home.

For a doll who had at one time been so loved, held every day and nurtured, one might understand her frustrations. She simply wants the life she had grown accustomed to with her dear friend. Pupa doesn't seem to be asking for any more than this as she has never displayed violent tendencies. By the reports from the family, the doll has never hurt anyone. She simply wants her freedom, and perhaps misses her dear friend.

Currently, and as far as anyone knows, the Pupa doll is still in the care of the woman's family. However, we have no way of knowing this for certain as no one seems to know where exactly she is. As such, there is little information to be found on this particular doll, past or present, and there are only a handful of photos available on the internet making her impossible to track down.

One can only hope that she is still being cared for and perhaps happily outside of her tiny glass prison, keeping her mischief under control. Perhaps one day she will resurface, and we might learn more of her story. Or perhaps she has simply moved on, reunited with her beloved friend on the other side of the veil.

MANDY

Mandy is most definitely a doll of mystery. No one truly knows where she came from; only that she was either made in Germany or England between 1910 and 1920. The only thing that we know for sure is that she is now kept in a Museum, located in Canada where she was donated by a woman who claimed that the doll had once belonged to her grandmother. Reportedly, the woman brought the ninety-year-old doll in, hoping to sell her as a valuable antique and because she was fearful that the doll was too fragile to be around her young daughter. However, after the museum took the doll, they found that perhaps the woman had been afraid of much more than the doll's fragility.

Almost immediately after Mandy was taken into the museum, she began exhibiting strange behavior. To begin with, Mandy was placed in a plastic bag, a standard procedure to rid her of any insect infestations that she might have had. Employees who worked in the same room where she had been kept during this decontamination period, claimed that they heard the bag rustling, though no bugs appeared to be causing this. They also witnessed the doll changing positions within the bag. They didn't quite know what to make of this, but soon realized that Mandy had many more tricks up her frilly sleeves.

Once the sanitation process was completed, Mandy was then taken for photographing and cataloging into the museum inventory. She seemed to behave during this process, but when the task was completed and the doll was left alone, her mood quickly changed. Employees returned to a room that looked as if a child had thrown a tantrum, scattering papers and other objects.

Trying to rationalize the odd incident, the staff decided to move forward and to give Mandy a placement near the museum entrance, hoping to make her happier. However, patrons soon began complaining that the doll was disturbing, with her tattered, old-fashioned dress and general disrepair. Although perhaps the creepiest feature of all was the doll's face; painted in a realistic manor, with life-like eyes and a violent crack to one side which caused that eye to bulge slightly. Visitors began blaming headaches and nightmares on the doll, along with a general sense of unease. Her disturbing presence was only the start, as employees of the museum began reporting the sound of footsteps after hours near where the doll was kept when no one else was nearby. They also pointed to the doll when electrical disturbances happened and when items were mysteriously moved from their original spot. The employees began to think that perhaps the spirit that was attached to the doll was unhappy, so they tried relocating her in the museum to appease the restless soul. Unfortunately, this only seemed to make things worse.

In their first attempt, and thinking that perhaps Mandy was lonely, the staff put her in a room with other dolls. This was very quickly realized to be a mistake. When they returned the next day, all of the other dolls had been torn up and damaged in various ways as if Mandy had gone into a jealous rage among them. Deciding that Mandy could not play well with others, she was then put in a room by herself. However, she seemed to grow even more distressed with her seclusion. She would have angry fits in the night which resulted in papers and other objects being scattered all over the room by the time the staff would return the next day. Employees began complaining of headaches and nightmares about the doll; and some even quit their jobs.

A psychic, wanting to help the spirit attached to the doll, asked if she might hold the toy in order to communicate with it. During this meeting, Mandy supposedly told the medium the sad story of how she had died in the cellar of an old farmhouse, still clutching the doll, her only friend in that lonely place. She told of how, years later, a man had been walking by the house when he heard a small child crying. He knew that the house was abandoned and so decided to check it out, in case a child had gotten lost or trapped inside. Upon entering the house, the man continued to hear the sound of sobbing, however, it seemed to be coming from beneath the floorboards. He could not find a cellar door inside the house, so he went back outside and located an exterior entrance to the cellar where he further investigated. Entering the dark storage space and looking around, the man supposedly made a gruesome discovery, finding the deteriorated remains of a small child along with her doll. It was not made known why the girl had been in the cellar; if it was by accident or if perhaps a crime had been committed. We also do not know why the man took the doll or how it came to be with its final owner before joining the museum.

After the psychic's revelation for the possible origins of the doll, the curator decided to contact the donor for more information. This is when the woman admitted that she really had just wanted to be rid of Mandy. She claimed that she would hear a child sobbing in her home and when she would go in search of the source, she would find the doll alone in her cellar staring up at her from the floor, and the cellar window opened yet again. After this had happened several times, the woman decided to be rid of it. She claimed to know nothing of where the doll had come from or if she had been found in the way that the psychic described with the body of a child. All she knew was that she wanted absolutely no part of it.

CHARLIE

In 1968 New York, a family made an interesting discovery in the attic of their Victorian home. Tucked away in a tattered trunk stuffed with old newspapers that were dated for the 1930s there lay a forgotten doll. The doll was clearly an antique, though its actual age is unknown. We can only assume that he came from the 1930s or earlier, with the only evidence being the dated newsprints tucked around him, and a tattered old piece of paper pinned to him with the Lord's prayer printed on it.

The family was pleased with the discovery as they were collectors of antique dolls, happily adding this hidden treasure to the rest of their collection and naming him Charlie. At first, they paid little attention to the new addition where he sat on the bench with the other dolls. However, when he started to move on his own, the owners began to observe the doll more closely. They began noticing that he would change position and location amongst his dolly comrades, along with other acts of mischief.

In the beginning, the parents blamed their children for the playful shenanigans. Yet, their five daughters adamantly denied having touched the doll, concluding that Charlie must be moving on his own—which left them understandably frightened. The parents dismissed the idea, until their four-year-old daughter spoke up, saying that Charlie would speak to her at night when she got up to use the bathroom. This gave the parents pause, but ultimately, they still dismissed the incident as a child's imagination running wild. They simply could not bring themselves to believe such a thing, especially since they had witnessed nothing of the sort for themselves.

However, whether the parents believed it or not, the doll continued to torment the children. The girls had become so terrified of the toy that they refused to leave their beds in the night, not wanting to pass by Charlie in the dark. Even during the daytime, they refused to walk anywhere near him. With all of this going on, the parents still denied the possibility that Charlie was anything more than just a toy—that is, until the four-year-old daughter came to them with scratches all over her body, claiming that Charlie had done it.

Finally taking the children's upset more seriously, though still skeptical about the whole thing, the parents decided to put an end to the chaos. In order to give the girls some peace, Charlie was taken back to the attic and locked away in the trunk where he had originally been found. Things calmed down in the house and thankfully returned to normal as the doll was once more forgotten.

Years later, when the daughters were grown, the house was put up for sale. They packed up their belongings and sold any unwanted items—including Charlie and his trunk. The doll was one of the very last things to go. A woman discovered him at the end of the sale and decided that he would make a nice addition to her antique doll collection. The previous owner warned the woman, telling her of their experience with Charlie, but she took the doll anyways. Oddly, the woman didn't seem worried about it at all.

From there, Charlie changed owners again and again over the years. He never seemed to stay in one household for long, and the stories surrounding him continued to grow as he was rumored to still be moving on his own, especially in the presence of young children.

This went on for many years, being passed from one family to another, until finally Charlie was donated to a little shop called *Local Artisan*. You can actually visit him here as he is on public display, surrounded by taxidermy animals, odd artistic creations, and other strange and unusual items.

The *Local Artisan* is located only ten minutes from Salem, Massachusetts, at 34 Cabot Street, Beverly, Massachusetts.

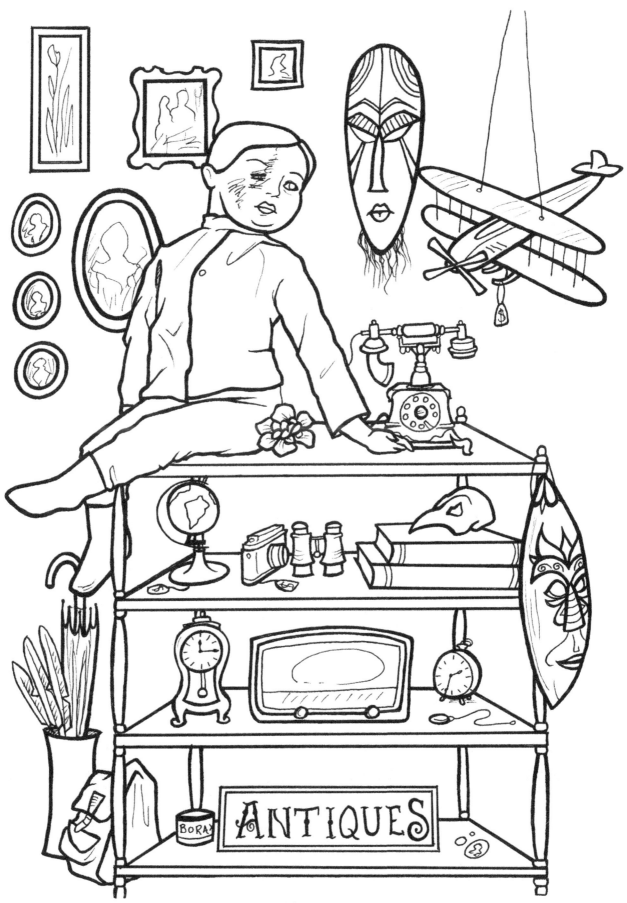

PEGGY

In 2015, Jayne Harris, a paranormal investigator in the UK, was contacted by a very distraught woman in need of her expertise. The woman told Jayne that she had come into possession of a doll and that with that acquisition she had begun having terrifying nightmares and nausea for which she blamed the toy. She went on to say that she had tried to relocate the doll throughout her house to ease the symptoms, but no matter where she placed the doll, the nightmares persisted. She claimed that she had also sought the help of two different priests, but neither had been able to solve the issue. She explained how both priests had left her home feeling ill with fever and hallucinations.

Ultimately, Jayne Harris decided to accept the doll, relieving the woman of her torment and with the intention of studying the supposed haunting for herself. Jayne immediately felt something unusual about the doll, so she decided to set up cameras that would record any possible activity. She posted the videos that she made online for others to watch and inspect along with her; the response was quite unexpected. Numerous people wrote to Jayne, claiming that just watching the video of the doll had made them quite ill with nausea, chest pains and debilitating headaches. One woman even reported having had a heart attack while looking at a photo of the doll!

People continued to connect with this haunted doll in various ways. Some claiming to have experienced flickering lights while viewing her videos, computers freezing, and the feeling that they were no longer alone in the room. Jayne kept a folder of the endless statements made against the doll by various people who had dared to watch her video or stare too long at her photos. She claims that the specifics of the haunting were not made public at the time, though the stories that kept pouring in were all very consistent in their similarity, leading her to believe in their validity.

Some of the more sensitive viewers reported having seen visions of what seemed to be a mental institution and the unspeakable abuse within. Others claimed to have sensed something similar; some sort of incarceration, a prison or asylum, possibly even something related to the Holocaust. One psychic medium went further, claiming that the spirit attached to the doll was actually named Peggy, and so she came to be known as such thereafter.

The story of Peggy spread quickly and soon became very popular in the paranormal field, eventually catching the interest of Zak Bagans, the host of *Ghost Adventures*. Peggy, initially with a black bag over her head and a crucifix around her neck, was featured on an episode with Bagans. The host was quite taken with her—even though she seemed to have plagued him with a small swarm of flies and feelings of fury during their interview. After the episode, completely entranced by this unusual doll, Bagans asked if he could add Peggy to his museum, a growing collection of haunted objects and oddities that he had been working on. After much thought, Jayne finally agreed and relinquished the doll into his care, feeling that it was time to let her move on. Peggy now resides in Zak Bagans Haunted Museum, in Las Vegas, Nevada.

The Haunted Museum is an 11,000 square foot building that dates back to 1938. In all of this space, little Peggy is reported to have her very own room where she sits inside of a locked glass case. The room itself is said to be closed and guests are given the option to enter at their own risk. If they choose to enter, they must agree to follow a certain protocol; they are to stand back at the marked distance, time within the room is strictly limited, guests must all greet Peggy upon entering and must say goodbye when they leave—after all, manners were very important in Peggy's day. Above all, guests are asked to respect Peggy in speech and deed; no touching, no referring to her as a *thing*, no sarcastic or demeaning remarks. She is quite easily offended, it would seem.

In all that has been recorded about the occurrences surrounding Peggy, we don't really know much about her history as a doll. We only know that she was made in England, sometime in the late 1960s, with no clue as to who the original owner was. Before Jayne Harris, the woman who owned her had simply found the doll at a sale, without knowing anything about who she had belonged to before that.

Peggy still resides in The Haunted Museum of Zak Bagans, where she can be viewed if you should ever decide to take that risk. Personally, I have looked at her photographs and videos without incident; however, I am always respectful when dealing with such things. Perhaps Peggy senses this and has left me in peace with my research. For that I am grateful and urge you to proceed with the same caution and utmost respect for things you may not wholly understand.

HAROLD

You've now read about a number of haunted dolls here within these pages. However, this next doll is a bit different. Where most of the previous dolls are simply said to be haunted, Harold's caretaker claims that this particular poppet is not only haunted, but actually cursed.

In 2004 Anthony Quinata came across Harold in an auction on eBay. He bought the doll along with a few other supposedly haunted items, hoping to write a book about his experiences with them. In the beginning, Quinata was skeptical, not really expecting anything to happen. However, his interest was piqued when the woman who had previously owned the doll tried to back out of the sale, saying that she was worried for Quinata's safety and that she felt guilty for putting this curse into his hands. Quinata insisted that a "deal's a deal"; so, the bargain was sealed, and the package was shipped out.

A short while later, Harold the doll arrived in the mail from Ireland. Immediately, Quinata put an EMF detector to the doll, curious if he could get a reading. The needle did not budge. Next, he tried setting Harold up with an EVP—again, nothing happened. It was disappointing, but Quinata shrugged it off, knowing that not every item he had acquired would prove to be truly haunted. Still, he would log all his findings in the book, as he had planned to give an honest account for each object. After determining that Harold most likely was not haunted, Quinata put the doll away in a box along with a crucifix and some holy water—just in case. You can never be too careful when dealing with these situations.

Several days later, Quinata decided to take Harold to a friend, April, who is very skilled in Psychometry. The visit was recorded on EVP, though Quinata had expected it to be the same as before with no response. He was surprised, after the session, to discover that the EVP had actually picked something up. As April conducted her session with the doll, she asked Quinata to take the doll away, saying that Harold was cursing and threatening to kill her, all the while unaware that the EVP had clearly recorded that exact threat.

In 2013 Quinata posted photos of Harold online and was flooded with feedback. People complained of sudden headaches and dizziness after seeing the doll. One person even claimed that she had awakened in the night feeling as though Harold was staring at her from within the shadows of her room.

The buzz about Harold continued until it reached the *Ghost Adventures* team and Zak Bagans. Curious about the claims made on the doll, Bagans contacted Quinata asking if he could take Harold on a little fieldtrip to The Island of the Dolls in Mexico. Quinata agreed, though he warned that the doll was quite fragile. Harold, it would seem, was a bit of a Frankenstein creation; comprised of parts from multiple dolls that had been manufactured sometime in the 1930s. And after all those years, the many implants and mistreatment, Harold had come to be very delicate, with one of his arms barely attached, cracked features and eyes that change from blue to black when Harold is angered.

Ghost adventures collected Harold for his little adventure, taking him to the Island of the Dolls, as planned (the episode is available online). They were careful, as promised, but at some point, Bagans had picked Harold up by the arm and subsequently suffered bruising on his own arm in the shape of tiny fingers. Apparently, Harold did not approve of being handled in this way.

After the show, Bagans took Harold to a local psychic, hoping to find out more about the doll. The psychic confirmed that Harold the Doll was most definitely haunted. In fact, he was haunted by multiple spirits that had been attached to the toy for many years. One of the spirits was that of a woman who seemed to be dangerously unstable, threatening to harm anyone who came near the doll. Another of the spirits was a man named Harold. Two others were Harold's nieces. And one was a demon. It is believed that the demon owns the doll, holding the other spirits captive within it—a troubling thought, indeed.

The list of atrocities and sorrows that have been blamed on Harold the Doll is quite long and ongoing. Many have blamed multiple ailments, deaths, freak accidents, nightmares and much more on the demon that dwells within the poppet. Quinata himself has experienced deaths and misfortune near to him, as well as three cracked ribs, which he attributes to the curse of the demon that is attached to the doll. As such, he takes his job as Harold's caretaker very seriously, with respect and proper documentation. You can watch Anthony's YouTube channel for a video diary of Harold and the activity around him.

To this day, Harold remains in the care of Anthony Quinata, even though he has been advised many times to rid himself of the cursed doll. Quinata's response to this advice is, "People *around the world* have been attacked by the demon within the doll. What good would it have done to put it 'outside?'". And perhaps he is right-- As they say, "keep your friends close, and your enemies (or demons) closer!

JOLIET

According to the folklore that surrounds this doll, Joliet has been passed down from generation to generation, from mother to expectant mother again and again. This would be an absolutely normal tradition, harmless even—that is, if the doll was not haunted *and* cursed. Supposedly, the doll brings the blessing of two children to the expectant mother, both a boy and a girl, respectively—as well as a curse that the boy will surely grow ill and die within three short days after his birth. It is said that the demon who controls the doll, traps the soul of each stolen boy within the doll's body, to remain there indefinitely.

If the stories are to be believed, this curse began with one woman, a very jealous and angry woman. Unable to have children of her own, the woman grew quite bitter when her friend announced that she was pregnant with her second child. The woman, who was mad with grief, felt that her friend was gloating about the pregnancy, rubbing it in her face that she herself was incapable of such a miracle. The woman tried to be happy for her friend. She even crafted a doll for the expected child. However, whether intentionally or not, she cursed every stitch as she made the pretty little dress that would disguise the evil that lie within. She poured every bit of her rage and ill-wishing into the poppet as she painted the face and readied the gift. The woman then took the doll to her friend, who named it Joliet and placed it aside for the expected child.

Finally, the blessed day came, and a son was born to her friend. He seemed perfectly healthy as he was laid into his mother's arms—his cheeks rosy, his cry robust. However, only three short days later, the babe was found dead in his cradle; the reason for his passing was never known. The child was taken away and buried, though it would seem he never left the home. The grieving mother swore that she was awakened many times by the sound of crying, only to find that it was coming from the doll, Joliet. She worried that the doll was evil, and at the same time, believed that the soul of her infant son was trapped inside—or that she was simply losing her mind with grief. Trying to dismiss the silly thoughts, she held onto the doll, tucking it away for safe keeping. She forgot about the toy and went on raising her other child, a daughter. In time, the daughter grew up and was married, eventually becoming pregnant with her own child. Now a grandmother, the woman remembered the doll and took it from its box, passing it along as a gift and in memory of her lost son—having forgotten all about the mysterious crying. It seemed that the curse was still alive and well within the doll, as the daughter gave birth to her own son who died only three days later. Again, a seemingly healthy boy, without issues, gone without any seeable cause. The daughter grieved for her loss, neither her nor her mother putting the two deaths together as anything more than a coincidence. The daughter, like her mother, was awakened to crying in the night, finding that the sound was coming from the doll. She thought that she must be going mad with grief, wishfully hearing the sound of her lost child. So, she wrapped the doll up and packed it away from her sight, never telling her mother of what she thought must have been a hallucination. The daughter went on to have a second child, a healthy baby girl who thrived and grew up into a beautiful young woman due to have a child of her own—and the cycle has continued in this way for four generations, adding yet another crying voice to the choir of infants within the poppet for every death.

Joliet now resides with a woman who chooses to remain anonymous, using the alias Anna for articles about the doll. Anna, like the other women in her family could never bring herself to part with the doll, feeling that her son and the sons from past generations were somehow attached to the vessel, or perhaps trapped within. And so, the doll remains with this family to this day. She has also chosen to remain in the shadows because no one ever believes her story of the cursed doll because—and this is eerie—only the women, specifically the mothers in her family can hear the cries of their sons. Only the women of her family are cursed and haunted by this sinister doll.

Not much else is known about Joliet. It seems impossible to find any further information on the doll or its whereabouts as Anna has chosen to keep her privacy, for fear of her daughter's fate when she one day has children of her own. Hopefully, Anna has tucked Joilet away in a box, hidden from any future generations who might stumble across the cursed doll and fall victim to this sorrowful curse—perhaps this is why she has kept her identity secret. We can only hope that this is the case and thar Anna will be the one to finally end the plague on her family, saving a future generation of sons.

If you have any further information on this or any of the dolls in this book, please feel free to contact me directly through social media.

THE ZOMBIE VOODOO DOLL

Magical poppets in various forms and by various names, have been around for many centuries, throughout many cultures around the world. Textual records in European history tell of the cunning folk in ancient times making poppets, with the intention of pricking them and thus harming the person linked to the effigy. However, the most commonly known reference to this type of doll has been made through the Haitian Vodou and Louisiana Voodoo dolls.

While some people who practice such things make their own poppets and Voodoo dolls, others have been known to purchase them custom made—or even *used*. But what happens when you buy a *used* voodoo doll? An object that has possibly harbored someone else's anger and vengeance, maybe even remaining with them until death.

One woman did just that! In October of 2004, a woman from Galveston, Texas purchased a used voodoo doll on eBay—and, as if being *used* wasn't bad enough, the poppet was also believed to be haunted. The buyer was skeptical of the previous owner's claims, not taking them seriously. So, when the doll arrived, she didn't hesitate to take it out of the little metal box that it had been sealed in. She had simply wanted to display her new artifact, but quickly found that this was "a real big mistake", as the woman admitted afterward.

The voodoo doll began by haunting her dreams, endlessly harassing her to the point of mental exhaustion. When she finally realized what was going on, the woman decided that she absolutely must be rid of this evil thing. She claims that she first tried to toss it into a fire, but it would not burn. Horrified, she tried to cut it up with a knife and scissors, but both broke without completing the task. Finally, desperately, she buried the thing in a cemetery, hoping to bind it within hallowed ground. It was sitting on her front porch the next day!

The original eBay seller's ad *had* warned that the doll was *very active*. The ad had also advised that the doll should be kept locked within the silver box at ALL times, never taken out or opened even to look at it. The woman who bought it, a novice ghosthunter, had disregarded the instructions thinking that the doll would make for a great investigation. Her initial motivation had been to disprove the doll as being haunted, thinking that the claims were most likely false. She quickly realized that she had been wrong and was in way over her head. She knew that she had to find a way to be rid of the doll.

Fearing for her safety and sanity, and as a last resort, the woman tried to resell the doll on eBay. Three times she successfully sold the doll, and three times the buyers contacted her complaining that the box had arrived empty— and three times she found that the doll had yet again found its way back to her front porch. She was even more terrified, feeling that this evil thing had decided to attach to her indefinitely, continuing its relentless harassment.

She eventually tried to contact the original seller for help, though the person never responded to any of her messages. Growing impatient, she decided that she would simply try shipping the haunted doll back to them. This did not work. The package was returned to her with the message, "resident deceased". At this point it felt hopeless; she had tried everything that she could think of to no avail. Eager for help with her situation, she began contacting paranormal teams with experience in haunted items, though none could devise a solution for the case. So, what was she to do? How do you get rid of a haunted doll that is determined not to leave your side?

After appearing on a radio show, speaking on the subject, a few callers suggested that she contact a priest and so she did. The priest came and she explained the situation, telling them of the incidents that had occurred and that he must not open the box. The priest agreed and blessed the box while keeping it locked. He prayed over the box, commanding the evil spirit to stay inside, never to come out and to cease its torment of the poor woman.

After the priest's blessing, the woman tucked the locked box away deep inside of her attic. She stated that her plan was to one day sell her house and leave the box hidden away, hoping that it would not be able to follow her this time. She has had multiple people offer to take the doll, but she claims that the people never show up or call her back.

As with any of the dolls in this book, these claims could be true, or they could be false. We can never know for sure. Either way, let this tale be a warning to you— DO NOT buy used, haunted voodoo dolls online!

THE ELUSIVE ONES

*These dolls were a bit harder
to find information on*

EDWARD THE TEDDY

EDWARD THE TEDDY

Our emotions and energy seep into everything that we touch, like a spiritual fingerprint, an echo from the past. This holds even more true for things that were touched during extreme emotional situations, and even *more* so when this is done during the actual making of an item. During the crafting process, rather than a simple fingerprint, the emotions then become part of the object's DNA. Of course, this is purely speculation by most scientific standards, though it is a firm truth for many believers. One such believer is the owner of a very strange and disturbing teddy bear named Edward.

Edward was crafted by a woman in England in the 1990's. The woman, name unknown, was said to have been in deep mourning for the loss of her child during the making of this toy. Tears rolled from her cheeks onto the bear, infusing the toy with her sorrows and bitterness for the world as her trembling hands did the necessary work. This may be the reason why people have felt overwhelmed with sorrow upon meeting the woeful bear.

It is hard to find the full story on Edward, or any photographs. However, from the scraps of information scattered on the internet, it is said that the bear has had a few owners, and each have been equally troubled by the toy. There are stories of the bear moving on his own, tormenting his keepers in their dreams and even causing them to suffer physically. It is said that there is actual video footage of the bear moving across the room, though I had no luck finding any such footage.

Where there was a shortage of information for Edward the bear, I had no problem finding a multitude of other haunted teddies. There is a tale of a small black chenille teddy from the early 1900's who the owner believes is still coveted by the little boy who once owned it. She came to this conclusion after multiple incidents, where some unseen force tried to snatch the bear from her hands. Then there is the account of Donnie the Bear, who is very possessive of the girl who owns him, scaring people out of her bedroom or making a fuss when he wants his mistress to return. And we can't forget Mr. Ted, the bear who talks. Snorting and growling on occasion, Mr. Ted also says, "no", and, "go away", along with other paranormal activity—very spooky! And there is certainly no shortage of haunted Teddy Ruxpin stories. I think haunted teddy bears could perhaps fill up a book of their own, however, we'll just leave it at this and get back to our traditional haunted dolls.

COMPOSITION

BOY

COMPOSITION BOY

Composition dolls were once quite popular in many countries: England, Japan, America, France, Germany etc. Made from a combination of wax, glycerin, glue and zinc oxide, these dolls are very heavy and dense in body; durability and weight being their signature quality. The exact mixture, or *composition*, was kept secret by each individual doll manufacturer, all competing for the best recipe. Around 1916, some dollmakers had even transitioned with the use of sawdust, or wood flour, in their mixture. This made for a lighter and more marketable doll, while still upholding the original claim that the dolls were virtually unbreakable compared to their porcelain counterparts.

These dolls were popular all through the early 1900's, finding their way into the arms of many children. One of those children was an 8-year-old boy, who had been gifted such a doll, which he quickly grew to love. He was so attached to the toy that he carried it with him wherever he went. We can only imagine the countless nights that this little boy whispered his joys and his fears to the poppet, his every secret. He must have held the doll even tighter on the night he died, reportedly from asthma-related complications. A sorrowful ending to a beautiful friendship and an all-to-short life.

The parents kept the doll, remembering how their boy had adored it, and soon realized that perhaps he was still attached to his treasured toy. One evening, glancing at the doll as they often did, both parents claimed to have seen the little boy standing next to it, silently, sadly drawn back to his home and to his little composition boy. The parents also claimed to have heard the little boys voice and footsteps near the doll on multiple occasions, as if he were still playing with his little friend. When these moments would occur, they also experienced electrical disturbances in the house—making the incidents even more notable.

This 100-year-old doll has been photographed in the past and even appeared on eBay multiple times, though his exact whereabouts are now unknown. From the photographs we can see that the little poppet was well loved by the physical wear on his face and body. However, no matter how faded and chipped his complexion might be, this doll's eyes are still staring wide and alert, watching everything and everyone around him—perhaps with his little master watching at his side.

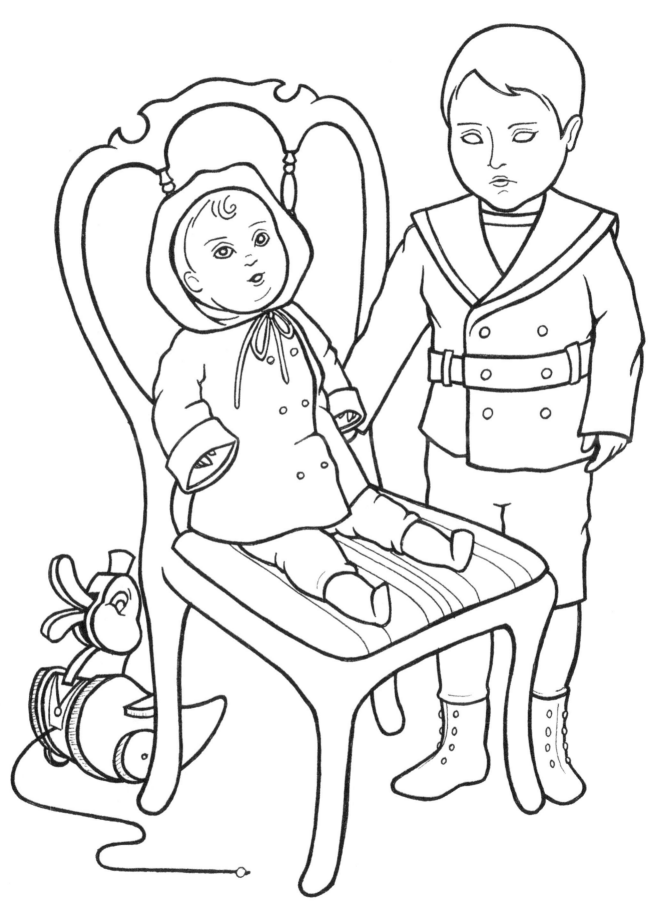

SAR'GOMOS

SAR'GOMOS

Most dolls greet you with bright and cheery eyes, their little painted mouths tipped into a friendly smile, beckoning for the playful company of children. They are the perfect illustration of joy and innocence, the epitome of youth. There is one doll, however, that was not made in this jovial fashion. Rather than having vibrant eyes and a smile, this doll's gaze is lifeless and dull above a mouth that seems to be forever frozen in a silent scream. It is a very unusual doll indeed, although his look of horror may be well-deserved if the owner's tale of possession is to be believed. They claim the doll is actually inhabited by an ancient Sumerian demon named Sar'gomos—now available on eBay!

This may sound a bit far-fetched for some—I mean, a demon? Come on! Don't they have better things to do than play with dolls? But the sellers have no doubts, having been convinced by the sound of screaming in the middle of the night and further by the demonic voice that came from the doll when they approached it upon inspection. The owner was terrified, also reporting severe electrical disturbances around the doll—and even the feeling of someone tapping them on the shoulder when they were near it. But then, maybe the little guy just wants to play? Screaming, flashing lights and then a tap on the shoulder—"Care to dance with devil?"

The current seller believes that the original owner or creator of the doll practiced dark magic, using the poppet to bind a malevolent spirit to the earthly plane. They also claim that the demon within the doll is named Sar'gomos. How they came to these conclusions is unknown, but even the vague possibility of such a thing is quite disturbing. However scary this thought may be, the owner does believe that the demon seems well-contained within the vessel, since he has not been able to do any real harm—yet.

Sar'gomos the demon doll has been listed for sale on eBay in the past; however, he seems to have sold yet again, as he is no longer showing in the search engine. As you might have guessed, this is not Sar'gomos's first go-around on the auction block. He has been listed multiple times and sadly has had a hard time finding a family that can handle his distinctive charms and talents. But who knows-- perhaps he has finally found his forever home!

If you have seen or know the whereabouts of this doll, please feel free to email me with any news or updates for his current haunts.

SALLY

SALLY

The story of the next doll begins with a child named Sally, who lived on a small farm in Massachusetts many years ago. As the tale goes, Sally loved her doll dearly, clinging to her in all things, taking her everywhere on the farm. She especially loved that the doll resembled her, with the same eye and hair color. The only difference was that the doll had shorter hair than she did—which made Sally want her own hair cut short as well. Her parents, however, would not allow this and so Sally reluctantly kept her long hair until the day she died at a mere ten-years-old. Tragically, the little girl drowned in a nearby body of water—probably still clutching the cherished doll as she took her last breath. How the owner discovered the doll's history is unknown, but the eBay listing says that they believe the doll to be haunted by this deceased child. And so, with this, the doll has come to be the namesake for this tiny soul, known only as Sally, the haunted doll.

Sally is a unique doll in that her eyes are forever closed, with faded eyelids giving the impression that her eyes are glazed over. A doll staring wide-eyed at you is disturbing enough, but one with white, dead eyes—now that's creepy! And, if the zombie-like eyes aren't enough to give you chills, the doll's short blonde hair also seems to *grow*—perhaps trying to look more like the little girl who haunts the toy?

The current owners claim that the doll's creepiness goes far beyond her unusual appearance and constantly growing hair. They have reported that this odd little poppet also moves! She goes from room to room on her own within their house, changing positions every time. They have even heard the sounds of splashing water and a child crying out from the room that the doll is kept in. Perhaps an echo from the child's tragic death?

This doll is most definitely not for the faint of heart. She carries with her a very sad and traumatic history that pains the heart deeply. A history that she repeatedly shares with anyone who is near her, plaguing them with nightmares of that fateful day—crying out in the night as she drowns again and again reliving the memory.

LACI

LACI

Tragic endings and haunted dolls seem to go hand in hand, as you might have noticed with a few of these stories. Strange disappearances, accidental deaths and mysterious endings have left many young souls clinging to the one friend they had trusted most in life. And while these tragic endings were painful to all who were involved, there is one that might be even more heartbreaking— the story of Laci.

According to the seller of this doll, Laci was a teenage girl. The girl had been raised by her mother, with her biological father being out of the picture. Laci had known her father as a little girl and had vague memories of him, which made her forever curious about why he had left. She begged her mother for information, wanting to confront the man, but her mother refused. She told Laci that he was a bad man and that no good would come from knowing him. Laci continued asking questions of her mother to no avail, though she found information on her father by other means and finally tracked him down.

With only an address, Laci set out to meet the man who had fathered her, against her mother's wishes. She planned to confront him, asking why he had done what he did to her mother and to herself by leaving them alone in the world. This had been her intention, though we will never know if she got the chance to ask her questions as Laci never returned from the trip.

Sadly, the grieving mother would never lay eyes on her daughter again, but her spirit—as all spirits do—seemed to have found her way home. Not all believe in such things, but many do trust that when we die, we gravitate back to the places and people who meant the most to us; to watch over them, or to say goodbye as we move on. The current owners believe that Laci came home and has stayed with the special doll that her mother had given her before she disappeared. The owner claims that you can speak to Laci and that she speaks back. However, they warn that the conversations are quite disturbing as Laci seems to know everything about you, even things that you may have forgotten or don't want anyone to know.

As if all of this were not creepy enough—Laci the doll's eyes are a dull red color—large and staring, watching every move you make.

RUBY

RUBY

The *Traveling Museum of the Paranormal and Occult*, created in 2014 by Greg Newkirk and Dana Mathews, is home to many unusual artifacts. Touring the world from one haunted location to another they have collected many bizarre items, one of which is the infamous and reportedly haunted Ruby the Doll.

Ruby had been a treasured heirloom for many years, having been with only one family for a few generations. She found her way into the museum through a friend of the curators, after her original family had begun to suspect that Ruby might be something more than a simple antique.

The family claimed that little Ruby would quite often move on her own, changing positions when no one was looking. They also reported that the doll would make strange and eerie sounds, though she has no voice box. Her family had also come to believe that Ruby caused headaches, nausea, extreme fatigue and other disturbing symptoms in people who were too near to her.

We don't really know for certain why or how Ruby came to be haunted, but it is rumored that a member of the family, a young girl, had died while clutching the doll. Knowing this, the family could not shake the feeling that their deceased relative might still be attached to the poppet. For this reason, they decided to request the analysis a psychic medium, though the woman failed to make contact with any such spirit. Apparently, Ruby can be a bit shy.

After the examination, the family tried to make peace with Ruby's disturbing history and tucked the doll away in their attic. However, even with the little poppet being out of sight, the thought of her lingered, forever haunting the family. After years beneath the dark cloud of this doll and her odd behavior, the family ultimately decided to relinquish Ruby to the museum.

In the care of the museum, Ruby appeared to calm down. She no longer seemed to make people feel ill and was never reported to move again. However, the curators did notice that their patrons seemed to be drawn to holding and rocking Ruby as if she were a real baby in need of affection. Many people have claimed to be overwhelmed with a maternal instinct in the presence of the doll.

Unfortunately, not much else is known about Ruby, only that she can still be found with the traveling museum. You can visit their webpage for tour dates at ParaMuseum.com or join them at Facebook.com/ParaMuseum

TED
THE CLOWN

TED THE CLOWN

Very little is known about Ted the Clown Doll. We don't know where he originally came from; only that he was once owned by a man named Ernest.

As the story goes, Ernest found the doll, perhaps at a yard sale or a flea market; that detail is unknown. Almost immediately after acquiring the doll, Ernest noticed that he was a bit different from the other dolls he'd known. He had an air about him that was both intriguing and unnerving. Ernest couldn't quite put his thumb on what it was about the doll—that is, until he left him alone.

When he came home with the doll, Ernest had placed the poppet in an upstairs room for safekeeping and then come back downstairs to go about his usual business. He was startled when he heard a noise coming from upstairs, as his house was empty other than himself. So, he went to the second floor to investigate and found that the doll was not in the place he had left him. Confused and maybe a little concerned, Ernest placed the doll back where he had been and went back downstairs. Again, he heard the sound of footsteps on the floor above him, and again he went and found that the doll had moved.

At this point, Ernest thought that he might be going crazy, so he replaced the doll yet again and *marked* the location. He then went back downstairs and waited. Once more, he heard the sound of feet walking across the floor. He waited, giving the doll more time than before, then went up to investigate. He was shocked to find that this time the doll had moved a full three feet! With this, he concluded that he was not crazy—the doll was simply haunted.

Ernest kept the doll, and over the years he continued to hear the sounds of Ted the Clown walking around in his room. He also began to hear new sounds as the doll came to feel more at home. The echoing sound of children's laughter would sometimes fill the air. It was a joyful sound, like children at a carnival, but it was also quite eerie as there were no children in the house.

Ernest tolerated all of this; the continual footsteps, the laughing, even the physical evidence where Ted the Clown's shoes started to look worn from all his walking. These things weren't so bad after all. But then the sounds coming from the room changed to a more sinister tone as the children's laughter changed to the sound of screaming in terror. And sadly, this is where all the information about Ted the Clown ends. Talk about a cliffhanger!

SHADOW DOLL

SHADOW DOLL

You may know of Ed and Lorraine Warren (now deceased) and the extensive collection of haunted items that they amassed during their lifetime, creating the *Warren's Occult Museum*. You are most likely, at least, familiar with one particular item in their keeping—the Anabelle doll. However, Anabelle is not the only spooky plaything housed in the Warren museum. There is also the lesser known, but equally sinister *Shadow Doll*—she may even be more terrifying than her raggedy friend.

Standing a few feet tall, the Shadow Doll is a very unusual creation. It is said that she is constructed of actual animal and human bone, with her hair being made of wiry black feathers. Her eyes are dark and menacing above a mouth that stays always agape in horror, as if screaming—some say, in readiness to devour your soul.

The origins of the Shadow Doll are not clear. The Warren's records only state that it was found by a couple in a small antique shop and purchased as-is. Soon after buying the doll, the couple began having terrifying nightmares and experiencing unexplained scratches on their body. Afraid of what else this evil thing might do, the couple relinquished the effigy into the care of the Museum. Upon inspection, the Warren's came to believe that this Shadow Doll had been used in Satanic rituals and that she harbored a dark energy. Because of this, they ordered that the doll should never be photographed or stared at directly. According to their records and various accounts, if one stares too long into the Shadow Doll's eyes or dares to insult her by taking a photograph without permission, they will have hell to pay. In retaliation, the Shadow Doll is said to appear in the trespasser's dreams, either causing a nightmare so horrifying that it brings on a heart attack and death, or at least a lifetime of fear and tormented sleep. The Warren's files claim that there have in fact been a few deaths that they believe were caused by the doll, and countless other people who are plagued by continuing nightmares.

Today the Shadow Doll still resides in the *Warren's Occult Museum* in Connecticut. Her beady black eyes are always watching and waiting for any who dare to come near the unholy collection—waiting for anyone who dares to challenge her dark gaze.

KATJA THE RUSSIAN DOLL

KATJA THE RUSSIAN DOLL

In Russia, around 1730, one of the Tsar's young mistresses became pregnant and was joyfully expecting her first child. She waited many months for the blessed arrival, as all mothers must, dreaming of the wonderful life the royal baby would have. And so, the moons of the year waxed and waned, bringing the date closer and closer until finally that fateful morning dawned, and the child arrived. Shocked gasps and looks of disgust, rather than smiling faces, swarmed the room as the newborn was passed to her mother. The Mistress was breathless, sobbing at the revelation that her precious infant had been born horribly deformed. Her heart was beyond broken for the poor child. However, the Tsar was more than heartbroken—he was furious and disgusted, immediately ordering that the abomination be destroyed by fire.

The childless mother, so filled with sorrow, crafted a doll in memory of her beloved baby girl. She secretly used the ashes of the child, carefully mixing the remains into the porcelain. She then gave the poppet the name that she would have given her child—Katja. The Tsar was horrified by such a macabre creature and ordered that it be destroyed as well. However, the clever mother invented a story that may not have been far from the truth. "Destroy my child again and you will be cursed!" she screamed in her mindless grief.

Fearful of any possible truth to the threat, the Tsar left the doll in the mother's arms. And because this fear of a curse lingered, so did the doll, being passed from generation to generation in Russia—fearing that there might be some retaliation if the poppet were destroyed or harmed in any way. She was posted for sale on Ebay once but was quickly removed as many weird and unsettling incidents began happening surrounding the doll, as if she refused to be sold in such a way. And so, the doll has remained in Russia, the mystery of her only growing with the many years that pass her by. One of the stories attached to this doll says that if you look into her eyes for 20 seconds, she will blink. And IF she blinks, something bad will surely happen to you in the near future—or maybe something very lucky, if she likes you.

The location of Katja the Russian doll is unknown, although she is believed to still be in her mother country. Sadly, it was quite hard to find much information on this particular doll, so I chose to creatively elaborate on the scraps of details that I did manage to find on her history with the royal family. If you happen to know more about Katja, please feel free to contact me.

SAMSON

SAMSON

Samson is a bit of a problem child, as haunted dolls go. His difficult and overly aggressive behavior seems to push everyone away. Because of this, he has been passed from one caretaker to another, having been on eBay numerous times with people simply wanting to be rid of him.

Samson has been described as very "jealous" and "possessive" of his caretakers, acting out when their attention is directed to another person, an animal or even another doll. No matter who he has been with, no matter which household he is a part of, Samson has been said to torment any animals or children that steal his owner's affections. In one case, he appeared in a baby's crib, though he had previously been in another room. When the parents tried to remove the doll, Samson grew angry; lights flickered, the baby mobile began spinning wildly and the rocking horse in the corner of the room began moving on its own. In another case, where Samson had grown jealous of other dolls in the house, he threw a tantrum destroying the other toys and throwing things around the room.

One owner made the effort to find out more about the mischievous spirit, in hopes of either helping or banishing it. The owner contacted a psychic medium who then came out for a private session with Samson. During the visit, the medium claims to have contacted the restless spirit of a young boy who was kidnapped, brutally tortured, and murdered around 200 years ago. For a reason that the medium could not uncover, the boy's bitter soul had grown attached to the doll and simply refuses to leave.

Perhaps this lingering entity, in his 200 years, had watched as children played with their dolls, growing jealous of the affection he had been denied in life. Maybe he simply wanted someone to acknowledge and play with him in the same way as those beloved poppets. It is possible that this is why he chose to attach himself to such a doll—maybe choosing this particular one at random, or perhaps he had a very specific reason. It would seem that there is much more to this story than the information the medium was able to acquire. As with many of these haunted dolls, we may never know.

THE
BLINDFOLDED
DOLL OF
SINGAPORE

THE BLINDFOLDED DOLL OF SINGAPORE

On a busy street in Hougang, Singapore, local residents were confused when they found a small doll leaning against a tree one morning, blindfolded. And, as if covering the doll's eyes wasn't odd enough, there was also an ominous message painted onto the fabric of the blindfold. It was a simple Arabic prayer, "In the name of God".

In the beginning, the doll seemed harmless enough, standing at only sixteen inches tall in her tattered satin dress. The people who found her assumed that maybe she had been left by mistake, simply a forgotten child's toy or maybe even as a joke. They had no idea what they were getting into when they chose to take the doll home, planning to clean her up, removing the blindfold. Soon after her blindfold was taken off, the doll seemed to come alive. She was full of mischief, causing her to be abandoned and found over and over again.

Owners of the doll claimed that she would move around the room when they weren't home. They also recalled hearing a woman's voice coming from the room where she was kept. And it was even said that she followed a few of the owners back home when they tried to abandon her, refusing to be left behind.

It is believed that the purpose of the blindfold was to trap the jinn or whatever evil spirit is inside. Each owner, at their wits end, would cover the doll's eyes once again and take her far away from their home. This seemed to be the only way they could be rid of her and keep her from following them back home.

Sadly, this is another doll that has scarce amounts of information available on her origin or current whereabouts. It has been rumored that the doll was made by an artist who specializes in making creepy dolls. Perhaps the artist is the one who placed the doll beneath the tree in jest; or perhaps the doll has a much deeper story that we may never know!

If you've heard of this doll and know any further details about her, please feel free to contact me through social media.

AMANDA

AMANDA

Designed by Heinrich Handwerck, Amanda the doll was made in 1984. Soon after her creation, a toy company in Germany began making many more dolls in her likeness, distributing them around the world. But the original Amanda was special to her creator, as all art is to its maker. The artist kept the doll in his family for many years— until one day she appeared on eBay.

Such a beautiful doll, it was not long before someone clicked on the 'buy now' button. However, the doll was very quickly rejected and reposted for sale. She has been up for auction more than 20 times, and each time the seller claims that strange things happen around this doll and they just want to be rid of her. They couldn't quite explain these strange things, only saying that the doll has some sort of power over the mind. One owner claimed that she grew obsessed with the doll and could not stop thinking about her; a complaint that other owners had also expressed. They each said that when they would lay down at night and try to put the doll out of their mind, it proved impossible. And that the more they tried, the worse they were punished with terrible nightmares.

One of the owners even claimed that she often found herself talking to the doll, confiding secrets in her. This woman also claimed to have been plagued with nightmares, and on one occasion she had even awakened to scratches on her feet. When she had first noticed the scratches, she panicked. She had even thought to call an ambulance, as her feet had looked so bloody and damaged. However, before she could dial 911, she looked at her feet once more and the scratches were simply gone, having completely vanished.

Amanda was investigated by Paranormal Investigator, Reggie Jacobs, who said that Amanda is actually a happy doll for the most part. She is just a bit mischievous when she gets restless. She enjoys playing wicked tricks on her current owner when she gets bored and ready to move along to a new home.

Amanda is now rumored to be in Atlanta, Georgia. She is displayed in a glass case in hopes of keeping her out of trouble, but the doll still finds ways to get under her caretaker's skin. She continually makes it very well known that she does NOT like being a prisoner in their display case and has grown quite bored and ready for a new adventure. People have reported hearing the sound of scratching and tapping on the glass, and the doll's position changes on its own.

EMILIA
THE ITALIAN DOLL

EMILIA THE ITALIAN DOLL

Over one-hundred years ago, in Italy, a porcelain doll of rare beauty was gifted to King Umberto by one of his most trusted soldiers and close friend, Ulvado Bellina. Sadly, soon after receiving this rare prize, the King was assassinated by Gaetano Bresci, the Italian-American anarchist. In remembrance of the king, the doll was given back to Bellina, who then gave it to his young daughter, Marie. Tragically, Bellina was also assassinated soon after.

Despite the tragedy that surrounded the doll, Marie treasured the beautiful poppet as a fond memory of her father. She lovingly named her Emilia and carried her everywhere that she went. She was probably the closest and most trusted friend that Marie had during such a tumultuous time. Together they survived the loss of her father, her king, two wars, *and* a bombed train.

Miraculously, Marie survived the train bombing, however, her precious doll lost both of her arms and her scalp in the explosion; her voice box was also damaged. These defects did not diminish Marie's love for Emelia one bit. She still adored the poppet that her father had gifted her; the king's favored doll. However, something did change between them after the tragedy on the train.

When the train was attacked, many people died, including one woman that Marie witnessed. Thoughts of the woman deeply haunted the little girl, so much so that she came to believe that the doll might be haunted by her. Marie claimed that she would hear the sound of weeping coming from the doll at night, though she no longer had a voice box. She also claimed that the doll would blink at random, without having been moved; and that her facial expressions would change very often to a look of great sorrow. And who could blame her? This doll has seen some serious tragedies in her lifetime!

Through all the misfortunes and the many blessings in her life, Marie kept Emilia and cared for her until the day she died. She even named her own daughter after the beloved poppet. Upon her death, Marie's daughter inherited the doll— and her mischief. The daughter claimed that the doll would move on her own, blinking and frowning when she was upset. She also heard the sound of sobbing coming from the doll in the middle of the night. Her voice box even occasionally coming to life, simply to say, "mama". It's really hard to find information on this doll, but one source did claim that she would soon be up for sale, though this has not been confirmed.

AMELIA

AMELIA

Amelia, like many troublesome haunted dolls, has been posted for sale on eBay quite a few times by multiple owners. Each buyer seems to have been lured in by her classic beauty and the promises of a haunting experience. However, when this doll actually becomes active, the buyers quickly change their minds and Amelia finds herself back on the auction block once again.

Like most dolls, this one looks perfectly harmless. Maybe even more so, since she is in good condition compared to some of the other dolls that we've seen in this book. Amelia wears a lovely lace-trimmed dress, with soft reddish-brown ringlets tied back in a lace bow; her face is painted in rosy life-like colors and her eyes are a joyfully bright green. All beautiful features, until you find out that those pretty green eyes had once a completely different color.

In her original eBay posting, Amelia had brilliant blue eyes and was claimed to be surrounded by supernatural activity. Curious if she truly was haunted, a collector purchased the doll for further inspection. At first, when she arrived, Amelia seemed to be just an ordinary doll, nothing special about her. As such, she was put away in a room, the claims of a haunting forgotten. That is, until one night when the man heard loud thumping coming from the room where Amelia was kept. Every time he would check on the doll, she seemed to have moved slightly. This was easy enough to dismiss--until it got worse. After going to bed one evening, he heard a loud thump against his bedroom door. Warily, he opened the door to find that the doll was right there *in the hallway*!

From there, the man claims that it only got worse. He continued to hear thumping every night, and one night he even heard giggling. When he went to check for the source of the giggling, he claims that Amelia waved at him with glowing green eyes. Her eyes have been green ever since.

Amelia has continued this behavior with all of her eBay buyers. Each one claiming to have had a similar experience. Each one being tormented by the constant thumping and Amelia's giggling, satisfied in her mischief making until finally they give up—placing her back on eBay.

ebay

Haunted

Giggles in the Night

Moves around

BUY AT
YOUR OWN
RISK

No Returns!

Glowing
Green Eyes

READY
TO
PLAY

AMELIA
haunted doll

BUY NOW
$ $ $

The Honorable Mentions

A FEW MORE DOLLS

NOT HAUNTED BUT DEFINITELY CREEPY

APPLE HEAD DOLL

APPLE HEAD DOLL

In colonial America, the settlers made an assortment of toys for their children using whatever they had available to them. Some of the toys, especially dolls, were often inspired by the craftsmanship of local natives who used corn husks or apples to make a quick and simple poppet that the children seemed to love.

Apple head dolls, like the one presented here, were made using a fairly simple process. First peeling the apple, the artist would then carve facial features into the flesh. The apple was then pierced through the core with wire and hung up to dry, with the artist checking in, to pinch and sculpt here and there as the doll took its final shape. It was often soaked in lemon juice to keep the flesh pale during its month-long drying period. Once the head was dried, it was adorned with hair, painted features, and other details before being attached to a wooden armature. This form was then padded with rags to replicate the shape of a body and then clothed in a handmade dress or pants.

It all sounds like great fun and totally harmless—not spooky at all—until you meet this particular apple head doll.

Made in the 1970's, the current owner bought this little poppet at the estate sale of a recently deceased woman, thinking to add the antique to her collection. She hadn't sensed anything unusual about the doll at the time, but soon after bringing it home she simply couldn't shake the feeling that something was off about it. She explained in one report that she could never bring herself to place this eerie creation next to her other dolls, claiming that this one had a strange and dark energy about it.

The owner has not reported any paranormal activity, but she does have a strong sense that the doll is haunted. Because of this, she was actively trying to get rid of it at one time, attempting to sell her on eBay. She could be right— the doll may very well be haunted—or it could simply be that apple head dolls are really creepy looking! Especially this one, with is shadowy featureless face.

Want to have a little extra fun this Halloween (or anytime really)? Look up apple head doll-making online and try creating one of your own. Feel free to send me pictures of your spooky poppets. I would absolutely love to see them!

PATTY REED'S DOLL

Patty Reed's Doll

Like many people in the 1800's, young Patty Reed's family decided to head out west to the land of gold and opportunity. Like everyone else, they were in search of a better and more prosperous existence during a time when life was hard and very often dangerous. They began their journey with the Donner party, departing from Independence, Missouri, making their way toward California in a large wagon train. Their hearts were so full of excitement and big dreams-- they had no idea how hard their travels were destined to be.

Not far into their journey, the weather turned quite bad, raining for days on end. This made it hard for the wagons to move forward through the muddy terrain. If they wanted to continue, to stay on schedule before their supplies ran out, then they would need to unload all nonessential items to lighten their load. Patty, only eight-years-old at the time, was forced to give up all her toys except one. All the children had to make this sacrifice, just as the adults made their own sacrifices. Each child chose the toy that was most special to them and keeping only that one. Patty chose her favorite doll.

Over the next year, this doll became Patty's closest friend and confidant, witnessing all of the harshness of the westward trail along with her; the brutal weather, the dangers of the wild and the deterioration of the wagon train. What had begun as a hopeful and joyous journey, soon became a sorrowful nightmare when half of their companions perished, and the other half were forced to partake in cannibalism in order to survive the merciless winter months. The horrors that this poor child witnessed were all fully steeped into the doll that she constantly clutched at her side.

This doll is not said to be possessed or cursed, but many say that to look into her faded black eyes is to see the death and sorrow of the many who perished around her. The haunted look of one who has seen things that no one should ever have to see. Chills run down your back as you lay eyes on such a creature, knowing what horrors and heartbreak it has endured.

Patty Reed's doll is now kept in Sutter's Fort State Historical Park Museum in Sacramento, California where you can visit her for yourself if you'd like.

THE JANESVILLE DOLL

THE JANESVILLE DOLL

For many years, driving through the town of Janesville, Minnesota, if you knew where to go, you would see what looked like a small child standing in the attic window of an old house. And if you listened close enough, or asked the right people, you would hear a multitude of spooky stories surrounding this strange fixture; this solitary doll of antiquity, that forever looked down on the town from his lofty room.

You might hear the rumors that the doll had been put in the window to honor a child who had passed away, leaving the poppet to echo the child's eerie cries into the night; Or that he belonged to a child who had been locked away in the attic, abused and murdered. Or perhaps you would hear the tales of how the doll could move on its own, changing positions and sometimes even running out into the night, chasing nosy people down the street. However, the true story of the Janesville Baby doll will not be known until the year 2176.

You read that correctly; that was not a typo. In 1976, the community of Janesville, Minnesota created a bicentennial time-capsule; a stainless-steel container that was placed inside of a stone marker. Each member of the community was welcomed to add their little piece of history to the vault, and many did. One of these citizens was Ward Wendt, the owner of the baby doll. Wendt claimed to have written down the true and secret story of the mysterious doll, sealing it with the rest of the town's contributions on that day, not to be revealed for two-hundred years. And so, the truth about the doll was tucked away for safe keeping. Beside this sealed scrap of paper, the only other soul who knew anything about the doll was Ward Wendt himself, a secret that he took to the grave when he died in 2012, at the age of 84.

After Wendt's death, the doll was removed from its perch in the infamous attic window and relocated to the Janesville Public Library. People continually travel from all over the world to visit the mysterious doll, drawn to him by the many stories—even though no one knows if the tales have any measure of truth to them. For all we know, this may be just an ordinary doll, a family heirloom and nothing more. He may have been sitting in that attic window simply for decoration or to scare away any snooping neighbors and trick-or-treaters, a great joke on the town. Or-- all of the hideous rumors could be completely true. I guess we'll just have to wait until the year 2176 to find out!

THE DOLL THAT AGED

THE DOLL THAT AGED

Dolls are generally made to be attractive, with plump rosy cheeks, bright eyes and smooth youthful skin. A plaything in the cheery likeness of the child for whom it is intended. This unique doll, however, looks more like The Crypt Keeper! His skin is shriveled and gaunt, his eyes are sunken in and beady, and his mouth is twisted into a malicious sneer. Most likely not the type of doll that you would choose for your young child.

To look at him now, it is hard to believe that this doll was actually quite handsome at one time. It was crafted to be a sweet-faced young boy, with his features painted in life-like colors, a cheery smile and joyful blue eyes. He was a beautiful toy years ago when the parents had bought him for their daughter.

Their daughter had excitedly unwrapped her gift, overjoyed at the new addition to her collection of toys. She deemed him 'perfect' and cherished the little poppet for many years, only putting him aside when she finally outgrew her playthings as a teenager. Then, like most toys, the doll was carefully packed away with other keepsakes and stored in the family's attic.

Years later, the family was cleaning out the attic, going through their old collected treasures, preparing to move. While sorting the space, they came across the box that the beloved doll had been stored in. The parent's, their daughter now grown, were excited to have found the old box as it had been such a fond memory for them all. Joyfully they opened the container, but their smile quickly faded into a look of confusion. Where the little boy doll should have been, there was instead a shriveled up little old man. His skin was crinkled, his eyes grown dark and beady-- somehow, the doll had aged!

Horrified by this grotesque poppet, the family donated the toy along with other unwanted items. They did take one photo before giving it away, as they thought no one would ever believe their story. And that was the last time he's been seen, his current whereabout unknown.

This mysterious doll, like the painting in the story of Dorian Gray, is simply unexplainable. Dolls, like painted figures, are not supposed to age in this way. Decay and damage are to be expected, but wrinkles? I think not.

LA PASCUALITA

LA PASCUALITA

For nearly a century now, people around the world have been lured to a little dress shop in Chihuahua, Mexico—although, not for the dresses. They visit, rather, hoping to view the mannequin displayed in the front window. Eerily lifelike, people come to decide for themselves if this is truly only a well-made dummy, or if perhaps something more sinister lurks beneath her painted smile.

La Pascualita first appeared in the dress shop window in 1930, soon after the shop owner's daughter had died. It is said that the doll bears a striking resemblance to the daughter who had died on her wedding day, having been bitten by a black widow spider. Because of the remarkably close timing and the uncanny resemblance, many people believe that the mysterious doll is much more than a simple mannequin and is actually the mummified body of Pasquala's daughter. The shop owner, of course, denied this throughout her lifetime, though the rumors persist. You can view close-up photos of her online at Ripleys.com and see why people so adamantly believe this bride to be more than what she is claimed to be. Her face, her hands, every feature is just too lifelike! And the resemblance to the daughter is absolutely uncanny.

The stories that surround La Pascualita have grown over the years. Some locals claim that a magician visits the bride at night, perhaps her intended husband. It is said that he pulls her from the display case and that they dance in the streets until sunrise, when he must return his bride to her window. If you visit her in the evening and then again in the morning, it is rumored that you will see her position has changed ever so slightly, her eyes following you.

One shop worker, Sonia, claims that when she must change the dummy's dress, her hands break out in a sweat. She says that the doll's hands are simply too lifelike, that the woman has veins in her hands and varicose veins in her legs. She firmly believes that the dummy truly is the embalmed and mummified body of the original shop owner's daughter—a true corpse bride!

While this is entirely possible given the right conditions, with perfect embalming, a controlled environment and very meticulous maintenance, most experts believe that this would not be the case in a little dress shop. The people most knowledgeable in this field, feel confident (although never 100% sure) that the mannequin is not a corpse and is simply a very well-made dummy with great attention to detail. We may never know the truth in this matter.

Atlanta's Doll Head Trail

ATLANTA'S DOLL HEAD TRAIL

When you go for a hike in the woods, the scariest thing that you would expect to encounter might be snakes or wild animals, maybe even a spider or two—but not creepy dolls. However, if you visit *Constitution Lakes Park* in Atlanta, Georgia, that is exactly what you will find.

Originally home to a 19th century brick factory that closed it's doors over fifty years ago, this 125-acre tract of land has since been reclaimed by the wilderness and by Dekalb County, Georgia. Abandoned clay pits have become manmade lakes; trails and boardwalks have been installed throughout the woodlands, transforming this abandoned industrial site into a beautiful wildlife preserve. However, tranquil lakes and trails are not the only thing you'll find lurking in these woods. *Doll Head Trail,* just as the name suggests, is a forest pathway tucked away within the preserve and littered with a parade of spooky doll heads, sure to send chills down your spine. Positioned creatively and disturbingly, you will see doll heads inside television sets, perched upon light fixtures and fans, nestled into the hollows of trees. Beautiful and sinister!

This trail began with the creative vision of local hiker and carpenter, Joel Slaton. Often walking through the park, Slaton started noticing quite a bit of discarded junk in the woods surrounding the trails: old television sets, discarded bricks, empty bottles and—yes--doll parts. One day, he decided to pull some of this rubbish from the woods to create an artistic display along the trail. It began as a little joke for fellow hikers to enjoy, but soon became the permanent theme of the trail as other hikers joined in. Over the years, many have continued to participate in the doll-part creations along the trail and Slaton encourages these contributions. He only asks that the elements used for the trail-art be park-found items and that the existing displays be left in peace, and to always keep your creations family-friendly--and just have fun!

Anyone can visit the trail; it's just a few miles from the downtown area in Constitution Lakes park at 1305 South River Industrial Blvd. SE, Atlanta, Georgia. Simply follow the trail signs from the parking lot to reach the Doll's Head trail. This truly is a great place to visit, whether you are looking for a peaceful nature excursion, or for a stroll with creepy dolls. There's even a public library display if you'd like to borrow or leave a book while you visit.

143

ABOUT THE AUTHOR

ABOUT THE AUTHOR

Born in Northwest Florida, Davina currently lives in Manheim, Pennsylvania. As an entrepreneur, artist and author, she has traveled all across the United States, collecting inspiration for her writing and art along the way. Davina's current publications include five educational coloring books, a handful of short-stories and an inspirational book for women. The complete collection of her titles can be found on Amazon.com.

In addition to her writing, she also runs a small local business and is the mother of two wonderful daughters. She loves being outdoors; camping, hiking, kayaking, traveling, open air markets, adventures of all kinds. She also enjoys oil painting and sculpture. She absolutely adores mountains and thunderstorms, fellow artists and writers—and all things creepy.

Davina attended Chattanooga State College, where she studied art and literature. These two subjects have been a constant passion throughout all her life; from elementary school to college and further continuing her studies independently through various seminars and classes. Her biggest literary influences have been Neil Gaiman, Stephen King, J.K. Rowling, Shirley Jackson, Susan Hill, Lewis Carroll, C.S. Lewis and Tolkien.

For more information or to contact the author, please join her at DavinaRush.com or on any of the social media networks below:

Facebook.com/DavinaRush

Twitter.com/DavinaRush

Instagram.com/DavinaRush_Author

Patreon.com/DavinaRush

A Special Thanks

So much goes into the making of my coloring books. The writing, the illustrations, the editing, and that little extra magic—my creative tribe.

My two daughters, Hailey and Melina are always part of the process from start to finish: their art critiques, our idea bouncing sessions, draft approvals, cover approvals. These two have been there for me through every single project I've ever done as an adult. They are the *reason* I began creating coloring books! I love you both so very much. I don't know what I'd do without you!

My sister, Trish, is also a big part of my work. We spend hours on the phone bouncing ideas back and forth for my projects as well as for her own (she also designs coloring books). For this book, she's the reason there is an "about the author" coloring page. I'd had the idea and was so excited about it, but when I started the illustration, I found it difficult and almost threw in the towel. My sister would not accept that—she pushed me to keep going, saying, "I *know* you can do this!" I love you sissy!

My sister from another mister, Jessica, has been my closest friend for over half of my life. We've been there for each other through, well—everything—including my writing career. She is always the final set of eyes to look over my finished work. This girl is a brutal editor and I love it! I can't thank you enough for your contribution and for the kickass office hideaway that you and Joe so lovingly provided for this book. You both are priceless to me.

Jason, who has been my best friend for over 10 years. This guy puts up with all of my crazy creative ramblings and always has some of the best input on marketing and media ideas for my work. He's been one of my biggest supporters and confidants through almost every book I've written. You rock!

Michael and Jessica, from The Grimm Life Collective, for being so supportive of my work and for all the fun movie nights that helped me to get through the homestretch of the illustration phase for my Haunted Doll book.

And last but certainly not least, Brandon. You have been such a driving force throughout this entire project. Your daily encouragement and excitement for the book, your selfless help in promoting my work, and the inspiration that your own book, "Vodou", provided for one of the illustrations, has all been invaluable. I am so grateful to have crossed paths with such a kindred spirit.

Patron Shoutout

They say it takes a village to raise a child, and I think the same goes for writing books. So many people have a valuable part in helping the process along. Sure, I could do it all alone—but would the finished product be of the same quality with only one set of eyes approving the work? Not at all.

In addition to those who contribute behind the scenes for the physical work, there are also those who contribute in other ways. Those who want to be a part of this dream by offering encouragement, direction, motivation and monetary support. I have been very blessed to have a few of these art-loving angels in my writing career; Brandon, Jason, Colleen and Franklin. I truly appreciate you four more than words can express, and I am really looking forward to continuing our unique relationship. I absolutely cannot wait to be sending you a copy of this book that we have all been so excited about for months! Thanks guys!

I would also like to send out a very heartfelt thankyou to some of the one-time patrons who gave me a huge hand up when the quarantine of 2020 hit. You all surprised me and deeply touched my heart with such a beautiful sense of community—my eyes are tearing up even as I write these words. Maureen, Diana, Robyn and Scott, Renee and Kyle, Swede, Jason, Mike, Shawn, John, Susan, Jessica and Joe, and Grampa Hal—from the bottom of my heart, thank you! You all made such a world of difference in this little writer's life, not only with the money that you contributed, but also with your friendship, your compassion and your belief in me and all that I do. You were there for me during an exceedingly difficult time and I will be forever grateful for your beautiful existence in this world.

"Throughout History, Ideas Need Patrons" ~ Matt Kibbe

If you would like to be a part of my patron tribe and receive the rewards that go along with that relationship, please feel free to check out my page at

Patreon.com/DavinaRush

Annabelle

Robert the Doll

Composition
Boy

Atlanta's Doll Head Trail

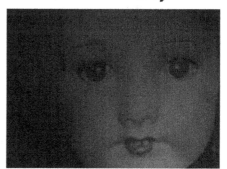

Amanda

Peggy

Sar'gomos

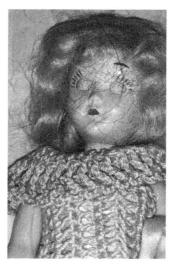

Sally

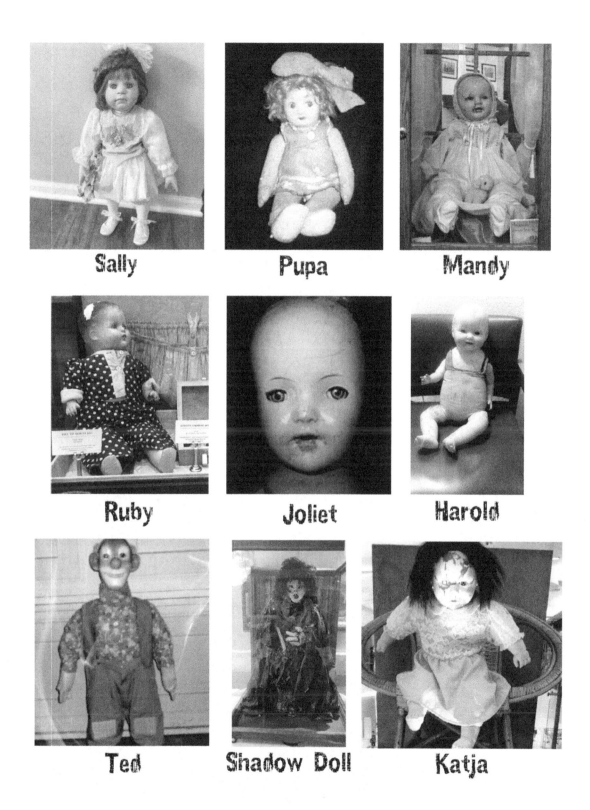

Sally

Pupa

Mandy

Ruby

Joliet

Harold

Ted

Shadow Doll

Katja

Emelia

Samson

**The Blindfolded doll
of Singapore**

Amelia

Apple Head Doll

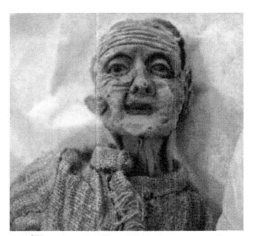

The doll that aged

La Pasqualita

Patty Reed's Doll

Doll Island

  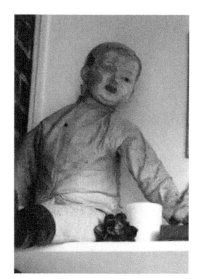

Letta **Okiku** **Charlie**

Zombie Voodoo Doll **The Janesville Doll**

Author, Davina Rush, around age 5

with the doll mentioned in the "Robert the Doll" section

Made in the USA
Coppell, TX
12 December 2021